SWAT
Secret World Adventure Team

Lookout London

by
Lisa Thompson

illustrated by
Nathan Jurevicius

PICTURE WINDOW BOOKS
Minneapolis, Minnesota

Editor: Jill Kalz
Page Production: Tracy Kaehler
Creative Director: Keith Griffin
Editorial Director: Carol Jones

First American edition published in 2006 by
Picture Window Books
5115 Excelsior Boulevard
Suite 232
Minneapolis, MN 55416
877-845-8392
www.picturewindowbooks.com

A
J.
Series
SWAT

First published in Australia by
Blake Education Pty Ltd
CAN 074 266 023
Locked Bag 2022
Glebe NSW 2037
Ph: (02) 9518 4222; Fax: (02) 9518 4333
Email: mail@blake.com.au
www.askblake.com.au
© Blake Publishing Pty Ltd Australia 2005

Printed in the United States of America.

Library of Congress Cataloging-in-Publication Data
Thompson, Lisa, 1969-
Lookout London / by Lisa Thompson ; illustrated by Nathan
Jurevicius.
p. cm. — (Read-it! chapter books. SWAT)
Summary: Will and Vika are recruited by the Secret World
Adventure Team for a mission in England, where they enjoy
many of London's famous sights while helping try to retrieve
a valuable family heirloom.
ISBN 1-4048-1672-0 (hardcover)
[1. Adventure and adventurers—Fiction. 2. Lost and found
possessions—Fiction. 3. London (England)—Fiction. 4. England—
Fiction.] I. Jurevicius, Nathan, ill. II. Title. III. Series.
PZ7.T371634Lop 2005
[E]—dc22   2005027168

Table of Contents

"It has to be here somewhere," said Will, searching under the bed. One of his in-line skates was missing.

"Doesn't look like it's in here," called Vika from inside the closet.

She moved a big pile of clothes and said, "I don't know how you find anything in this place. Maybe if you cleaned up you'd find it."

"Look, I know you're not going to understand, but I know where everything is when my room is like this," said Will.

"So where's the skate? Don't tell me—it rolled away without us?" said Vika, widening her eyes.

"Very funny," said Will. "You know, I'd find it a lot faster if you helped me instead of goofing around." He kicked over a stack of magazines.

"I AM helping you," said Vika, reaching over the mess on his desk. "What's this thing for anyway?"

Will put down the smelly old sports bag he was searching through and said, "I don't know. I've never seen it before in my life. Let me take a look."

Vika was holding a plastic device that was flashing and beeping. Then, it spoke.

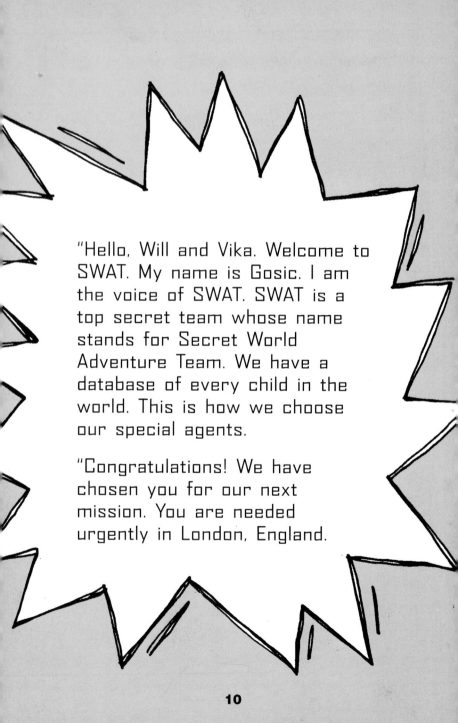

"Hello, Will and Vika. Welcome to SWAT. My name is Gosic. I am the voice of SWAT. SWAT is a top secret team whose name stands for Secret World Adventure Team. We have a database of every child in the world. This is how we choose our special agents.

"Congratulations! We have chosen you for our next mission. You are needed urgently in London, England.

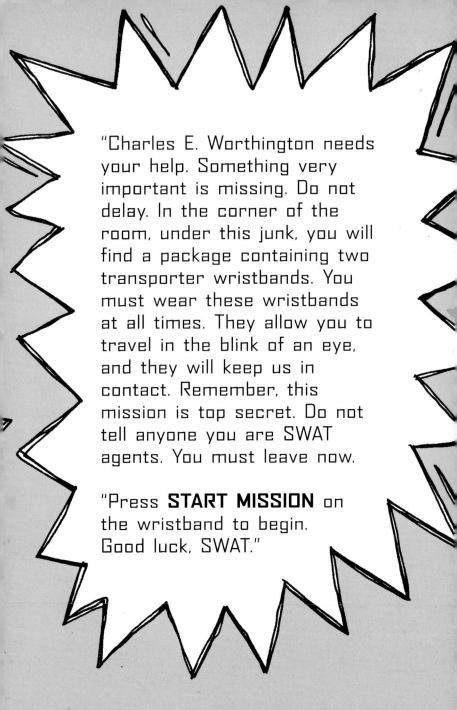

"Charles E. Worthington needs your help. Something very important is missing. Do not delay. In the corner of the room, under this junk, you will find a package containing two transporter wristbands. You must wear these wristbands at all times. They allow you to travel in the blink of an eye, and they will keep us in contact. Remember, this mission is top secret. Do not tell anyone you are SWAT agents. You must leave now.

"Press **START MISSION** on the wristband to begin. Good luck, SWAT."

The device stopped flashing.

Vika jumped toward the pile of junk in the corner, found the package, and ripped it open.

"Forget the skate, Will. We're off to England," said Vika.

She held out a wristband for Will to put on.

"I can't believe Gosic called that a pile of junk," said Will.

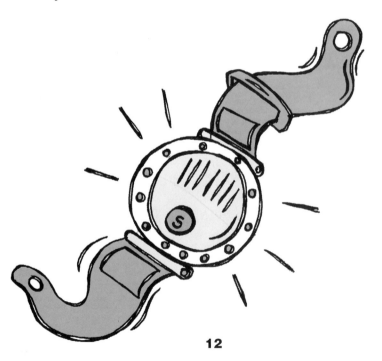

Vika shook her head. "Gosic is right. It IS junk," she said.

Will sighed. "So, how do these things work?" he asked, looking at his strange wristband.

Vika flicked through the SWAT instruction manual and said, "All we have to do is count down from three and press **START MISSION**. Three. Two. One."

Click.

CHAPTER 2

London Rooftop

Exactly one dizzy second later, they landed on the roof of an Edwardian house looking down over central London.

"Wow!" cried Vika. "We're in London—Europe's biggest city!"

Modern towers of glass and steel broke up the skyline of old buildings and church steeples.

Vika jumped up and down, pointing. "There's St. Paul's Cathedral, and over there are Big Ben and Westminster Abbey," she cried.

"Quiet," said Will. "I think I heard something."

They were not alone. A girl with spiked hair, a pierced nose, and big boots was standing nearby, shouting at a boy.

"How could you be SO stupid, Charlie?" she yelled. "Didn't you check before you gave it to him? I mean, it has been in the family for hundreds of years. Dad is going to FREAK!"

Charlie was sitting with his head down, looking into an empty box. The girl leaned over him. Her big black boot stomped loudly right next to him.

Will and Vika were frightened. They hid so they wouldn't be seen.

The girl continued, "At 6 P.M. tonight I want to see it back in its box, little brother. Otherwise, I'm going straight to Dad, and then you'll be in MONSTROUS trouble, Charles E. Worthington! It's what you deserve."

She gave a short, mean laugh and walked away.

Charlie just sat there, trembling.

"Are you OK?" Will asked, walking over. "Your sister is really scary."

"Will, don't say that," said Vika, coming out to join them.

"You heard her?" asked Charlie. He looked very shaken.

"I think half of London heard her," said Will, rolling his eyes.

Charlie's face turned even whiter.

"Charlie, I'm only joking," said Will.

"She's OK," said Charlie. "She's just angry. But not half as angry as Dad's going to be if I don't get it back." Charlie shook the empty box. "How could I have been so stupid?"

"What did you do?" asked Vika, looking out over the buildings.

"We had a pendant of our family crest," explained Charlie. "It has been in our family for centuries. It's worth a fortune. I traded it with a boy for tickets to a football—er, I mean 'soccer'—match. Box seats to the FA Cup Grand final. They're almost impossible to get."

Charlie held up the tickets.

"You did WHAT?" asked Will and Vika.

Charlie looked flustered. "I didn't know I was trading the real one. We have a fake one that we usually keep on display. It's worthless, but it looks like the real thing. I thought I was trading that one."

"You got them mixed up," said Vika, putting her hand over her mouth. "That was a big mistake!"

"It has to be in this city somewhere," said Will. "Charlie, we'll help you get it back. I mean, we're looking for something that's one of a kind, right? How hard can that be?"

Charlie looked relieved. He didn't even bother to ask why Will and Vika were on the roof. Perhaps he thought it best not to know. He ran downstairs to get the fake pendant.

"We have to find Charlie's pendant before his dad finds out," said Vika quietly.

Will and Vika needed to think of a plan.

CHAPTER 3

Where Do We Begin?

The weather was windy and gray as they waited on the rooftop.

"Here it is!" said Charlie, out of breath from running up the stairs.

The fake pendant looked amazing.

"That's the most beautiful thing I've ever seen!" Vika gasped.

Even Will had to admit it was impressive.

"OK, Charlie. Any idea where the real pendant might be now?" asked Will.

Charlie shrugged and said, "In a city of eight million people, it could be just about anywhere."

He continued, "The guy I traded with sometimes sells theater tickets at the West End. Maybe if we go there, we'll see him."

"It's worth a shot," said Will. "At least it's a start. Let's climb down to the street and get going."

"It won't take us long," said Charlie. "The West End isn't far."

As they walked along the tree-lined streets to the city, they passed rows of terrace houses. Charlie told them all about his family's history and how they have lived in England for centuries.

"I'm the eighth Charlie E. Worthington in our family," he said. "How about you?"

"I'm the first Will in my family," said Will.

Charlie looked unimpressed.

"Oh my gosh!" Vika exclaimed. "Is that Buckingham Palace?"

"You ARE new to London," said Charlie with a grin. "Yes, it's the Queen's palace. She's not home today. The flag is down."

Vika ran to the gate and squeezed past the tourists to make her way to the front. Will and Charlie followed.

It was time for the changing of the guard. The palace guards were dressed in red jackets and tall, furry hats.

As the old guard gave the keys of the palace to the new guard, their faces were very serious. Will tried to make them laugh by making funny faces.

"It won't work," said Charlie. "They are trained not to react to you. I've tried it a million times myself. Let's cut across St. James Park."

They both made one last face before they turned away.

The park was calm, orderly, and very beautiful. There were people feeding ducks, sitting on benches, listening to cricket matches on the radio, and reading the paper. Others were performing for passers-by or playing soccer.

"Do you play soccer, Charlie?" asked Vika.

"Sure! Although we call it 'football.'
This season I scored the second
most points on my team!" he
said proudly.

"Who scored the most?" asked Will.

"My sister," said Charlie.

Will laughed. "That figures!"

Once across the park, they took a shortcut through some old, narrow streets. They came out at a lively place called Piccadilly Circus.

"This part of the West End is the world's theater capital," said Charlie.

There were signs everywhere saying what was playing, what was coming, and who was starring. It was a busy place filled with restaurants, cafes, and theaters. Charlie, Will, and Vika walked over to a half-price ticket booth. The lady inside recognized Charlie right away.

"Hello, young man. The boy you traded with seemed very happy. I can't believe he traded those fabulous tickets! I've been trying to get them for ages! How on Earth did you do it?" she asked.

Charlie paled.

"Do you know where he is now?" asked Will.

"Hmm. I talk to so many people every day. Let me see. I think he did mention something about going down to the markets at Portobello Road," she said.

Quick as a flash, they were off, running toward the market.

"Let me know if you want to trade, Charlie!" she shouted after them.

CHAPTER 4
The Market

The market was packed when they arrived.

"This looks like a great place to find a bargain," said Vika.

"There are so many places the pendant could be. It's such a mess. We'll never find it!" Charlie was in a panic.

Will didn't see it that way. "Frankly, Charlie, I like it when things are like this. The messier the better, I say."

"Just like your bedroom!" said Vika, rolling her eyes and shaking her head.

They rushed down more narrow streets and came to a very interesting shop. The sign above the door said, "E.E. Simmons Antiques—Quality Traders for Centuries." The shop was packed with all sorts of weird, wonderful old stuff.

There were huge chairs that looked like they belonged to the Queen. The best collection of ugly vases Will had ever laid eyes on was next to some strange sculptures. Will, Charlie, and Vika stopped in their tracks at the sight of a huge, growling stuffed dog.

"How awful!" said Vika, as she bared her teeth back at the dog.

"Madam," said a very proper man in a pair of horn-rimmed glasses, "some people like stuffed animals."

Vika rolled her eyes.

"Actually, we're trying to find a pendant that looks exactly like this one," Will said, as he held up the fake pendant.

"Extraordinary," said the shopkeeper. "Very, very interesting. But I'm afraid I haven't seen it. I would certainly have remembered such a beautiful and unique piece. Maybe you could try the markets down the lane."

The three of them ran off down the lane.

The market was buzzing with traders. It seemed like everyone had a bargain.

"Never mind 35. Forget 25! I'll give you the bargain of your life and slice and dice the price to 10!" one trader yelled.

Another yelled, "Too late! Too late I hear you cry. The fella with the bargains has passed you by!"

"I'll throw in not one, not two, but three for the price of one. You won't find a better deal than that in all of London," cried another.

It seemed you could get almost anything at the market, but unfortunately, no one had seen Charlie's pendant.

Charlie was losing hope.

"Don't worry, Charlie. Finding things takes time," said Will.

"We haven't got a lot of time," said Charlie glumly. "It's already lunchtime."

"So it is," said Will. "I bet if we eat, we'll find it more quickly. You've certainly heard of 'brain food,' haven't you?"

"'Brain food'—ha! You're ALWAYS hungry," said Vika, shaking her head.

It was hard to decide what to have for lunch. Will wanted fish and chips, but Charlie wanted tea and scones.

"Tea and scones! You must be joking," cried Will.

"Scones with lots of jam and cream will make me worry less," said Charlie, patting his stomach.

"Hmm, a pot of tea and some scones," said Vika. "I'll have some, too. Then I can pretend I'm having tea with the Queen," she laughed.

"I'll stick with fish and chips," said Will.

They went down to the River Thames and ate lunch. They stood on Waterloo Bridge and took in the view of the city. Charlie pointed out some of the sights, such as the Houses of Parliament and the Tower of London. Being a tour guide seemed to cheer Charlie up. They counted red double-decker buses and black cabs in the traffic.

The "brain food" seemed to help, because Will finally had an idea.

CHAPTER 5

The Underground

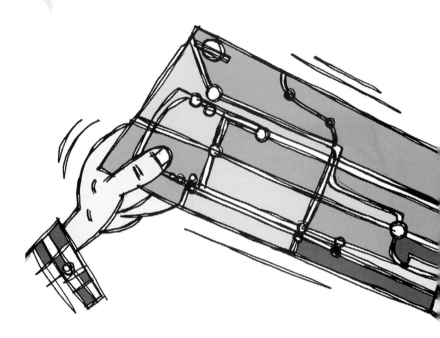

Will had a theory. He thought that if you really wanted to find something, you stopped looking for it, and then it would turn up. Charlie wasn't sure, but seeing that no one else had a better idea, they decided to try out Will's theory.

"What is this other thing we are going to do?" asked Vika.

"Let's go and ride the Underground," said Charlie. "I love riding on the trains. You see all sorts of people."

The Underground is the name of London's rail system. It's called the "Underground" because that's where it is mostly—underground.

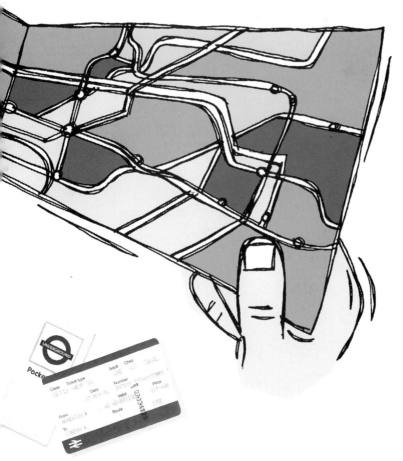

"Let's ride the yellow line," said Charlie.
"That's the train that goes around the city.
It's my favorite."

Charlie was right. There were certainly lots
of interesting people to see and to meet.
They met a lady who was overloaded with
boxes from a day of shopping.

"I bought this hat for the race!" she said.
"What do you think? And I bought these
gloves for gardening. And this is for polo."

They chatted with an artist who had spent the morning at the Tate Gallery.

"Such fantastic color!" he cried. "Such interesting use of light. Such imagination!"

They watched a man in a very flashy suit scan his newspaper with a worried look.

Then they listened to a group of people talk about a party they had been to over the weekend.

"I love that DJ. Don't you think he plays the best music?" one of the girls asked.

They jammed with a group of street
performers from Morocco and then got
off the train.

CHAPTER 6
The Real Pendant

Will, Vika, and Charlie walked out of the station and into the park. Suddenly, Charlie stopped.

"Wait a minute!" he said. "This is where I first met him. The boy with the pendant."

"Are you sure?" asked Will.

"Positive. I remember the grandstand."
Charlie pointed to the stands. "That's
where he was sitting."

At the other end of the park was a bus
stop. A boy was waiting for a bus.
Charlie squinted and covered his eyes.

"I think that's him," said Charlie. "That's
the boy with my pendant."

"Are you sure?" asked Will.

Charlie nodded.

There was no time to explain. Will and Vika grabbed Charlie by the arm and hit the button on their wristbands.

"Three. Two. One," they said.

Click.

When they arrived at the other side of the park, Will yelled, "Stop! Wait!" The boy was about to get on the bus.

The boy turned around. "Hey, I've been looking for you!" he said to Charlie. "My big brother FREAKED OUT when he found out that I had traded the tickets. I'm in trouble. I was wondering if ...." The boy looked down at the ground. "I was kind of wondering if you'd be interested in trading them back."

Charlie said, "I don't know. They are pretty amazing tickets."

What on Earth was Charlie doing, wondered Vika and Will. OF COURSE Charlie wanted to trade the tickets back!

The other boy looked disappointed and said, "Look, I know they're awesome tickets. But I really need them back. I'll tell you what. How about if I give you three tickets to tonight's match? They're the best seats in the house!"

The boy pulled the pendant and the tickets out of his pocket. The pendant was 10 times more amazing than the fake one. Will and Vika had to keep their jaws from dropping.

"I really need those tickets back," he said.

Charlie pulled out the tickets and traded with the boy.

"Thanks. Thanks a million. You've just saved my life," said the boy. "Gotta run. See you!" The boy was still grinning from ear to ear as he ran up the street.

CHAPTER 7

Completing the Mission

"Charlie!" said Vika. "What were you doing? I almost thought you weren't going to trade!"

Charlie gave a sly smile. "Well, they were EXCELLENT tickets, Vika. I couldn't just hand them back."

Will held up the pendant. "Let's take this back right now before anything else happens to it."

"Say," said Charlie, "how did you guys get us across the park so quickly?"

"Um," said Vika, as Will counted down, "like this. Three. Two. One."

Click.

They were back on the roof of Charlie's house in a flash.

"How did you do that?" asked Charlie.

Vika stumbled for the words. "Well, um, you see we ...."

"Charlie! Is that you? Who are you talking to?" Charlie's sister climbed the stairs to the rooftop doorway.

Will and Vika ran and hid.

"I was, um ...," stammered Charlie.

"So I guess I can go and get Dad, huh? Fill him in on your little disaster," she said with a mean grin.

"No need," said Charlie, triumphantly holding out the pendant. "Here it is."

His sister's eyes grew so wide they looked as though they might pop out of her head.

"How in the world did you get it back?" she cried.

"Easy," said Charlie. "I just didn't look, and it turned up by itself."

"I don't believe it!" she said. "This is amazing! I don't know how you did it, Charlie, but I'm amazed!" She took the pendant and put it in the box. "I'm going to put this back where it belongs right now."

"And," said Charlie, whipping out the tickets, "I have tickets to tonight's football match for Dad, you, and me."

She looked at the tickets and cried, "This is fantastic. I've got to tell Dad. We have to get ready! We have to go!" She ran downstairs screaming, "Dad! Dad! You're never going to believe this! Hey, Dad! DDDAAAAADDD!"

Then she raced back onto the roof and yelled, "Come on, Charlie! What are you doing? Quick, we have to get ready!"

Charlie gave Will and Vika a wave and whispered "thank you" before he turned and followed his sister downstairs.

Will and Vika felt their wristbands vibrate. It was a message from Gosic:

Congratulations, SWAT! Mission successful.

Then, a button magically appeared marked **MISSION RETURN**.

"Well, I guess that's it," said Vika. "Time for us to go home. I must say I'm very impressed with your theory, Will."

"Yeah," he chuckled. "Too bad it didn't work for me with my skate."

"I bet I'll find it when we get back," said Vika with a huge smile.

"You mean, you know where it is? Where?" cried Will.

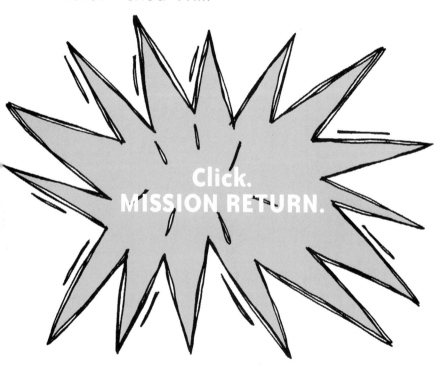

Click.
MISSION RETURN.

"Here you are—one in-line skate," Vika said, holding it up triumphantly.

"Where was it?" asked Will.

"In your football bag. And just think— we had to go halfway around the world to find it," laughed Vika.

GLOSSARY

Buckingham Palace—home to the Queen of Great Britain

cathedral—a large, important church

chips—British word for "french fries"

cricket—a bat and ball game

Edwardian—from the period of Great Britain's King Edward VII (reigned 1901–1910)

FA Cup—a famous soccer competition in England

family crest—a family's coat of arms, or symbol

horn-rimmed—made of animal horns or tortoiseshell

pendant—an ornament on a necklace

Piccadilly Circus—a major traffic intersection in London

scones—pastry-like breads, usually cut into triangular shapes

St. James Park—the park opposite Buckingham Palace

Tate Gallery—a famous art gallery in London

terrace houses—tall houses that are joined at the sides

theory—an idea about something

Underground—the underground train system in London

unique—one of a kind

West End—the famous theater district in London

IT COULD BE YOU!

Secret World Adventure Team

COME
TRAVEL
TODAY!

A complete list of *Read-it!* Chapter Books is available on our Web site:
www.picturewindowbooks.com